Devotions & Prayers to Anchor the Soul

Anecia B. Lee

Foreword

In the book "Devotions and Prayers to Anchor the Soul" Anecia Lee pours out her compassion and love for Jesus and others. The devotions guide the reader into the depths of God's Word, bringing out the need to just Be Still and find peace in His goodness and wisdom. Paired with the devotions, each prayer is in its raw and original prayed state and can serve as a heart cry to the Lord very much like the Book of Psalms. Just as King David prayed personal and deeply emotional prayers to the Lord, Anecia's gift of worshiping God with the art of prayer will bring her readers to their knees. As a devoted child of God, wife, mother, grandmother, and friend, Anecia is able to intercede on behalf of others in a way that leaves their deepest needs on the alter before our merciful Lord Jesus. As a wise and gifted counselor, Anecia sees deeper into prayer requests of others than just the initial ask. Anecia's love for God is felt in her praise and thanksgiving and her ability to speak light and life into the darkest moments is a joy to read and pray along with. May each reader receive a blessing and an encouragement to bare their souls before God in Spirit and in truth.

- Kelley Jean Blas

Dedication

I dedicate this work first and foremost to Jesus Christ, my Lord and Savior. He is the One who called, gifted and challenged me to be obedient to His Voice. I am who I am because of Him.

To my husband, Roger who was faithful to listen and encourage me to take what God was saying and put it on paper. Roger, you were always willing to help me visually see things as I was trying to put pictures into words. I love you more than words can ever express. Thank you for believing in me and being my greatest cheerleader.

To my sons Blane and Jonathon whom I love with my heart. These two encourage me to be a better mom and Woman of God. May I always point you to be lovers of God.

To Deanna and Taylor, the girls who stole my Sons heart and mine. I love encouraging you as the Wives to my sons and moms to my treasures. I pray I am always an example and point you to Jesus.

To my Treasures, the beauties God blessed me with. Ella Grace, Adalyn Ruth and Lainey Olivia.

Ella Grace, you are amazing. I am so excited to see how God grows you into the person He has called you to be. I pray you love Him with your entire being.

Adalyn Ruth, you are as equally amazing. God is moving in your life already as you pray and speak to him. I look forward to seeing where He takes you. Love Jesus with your entire being.

Lainey Olivia, Father is still forming you in mother's womb. What a blessing you have been already and I look forward to your arrival. As you continue growing in Jesus, I am excited to see what He is up to with you. To my family, thank you for your love and support throughout my life.

To my Dad in heaven. You always pushed me to be the best in all I did. I am forever grateful for and to you. Thank you for all you have instilled in me, to include, "this Christian walk is simple Neci, it's simple."

Acknowledgement

Thank you to all who have supported and prayed for me as I have worked on this devotion and prayer book. To those who read over my devotions and offered your input, corrections, prayers, and thoughts.

To my niece Brandi who so graciously transcribed all my prayers from audio files.

To Lorena who worked tirelessly to create a beautiful devotion and prayer book with just the right touch.

Thank you to Jerry and Stephanie for the beautiful beach scene which adds to the peace offered inside the book.

To my husband, who prayed over me faithfully from beginning to end.

To my sons who graciously gave me permission to include the blessing that I prayed over them in this book.

Finally, to Father, who I owe my ALL to, for speaking each devotion and prayer into my spirit and asking me to join him in writing and praying.

The God Who Heals
(Jehovah Rapha)
Luke 8:43-48 (KJV)

43   And a woman having an issue of blood twelve years, which had spent all her living upon physicians, neither could be healed of any,

44   Came behind him, and touched the border of his garment: and immediately her issue of blood stanched.

45   And Jesus said, Who touched me? When all denied, Peter and they that were with him said, Master, the multitude throng thee and press thee, and sayest thou, Who touched me?

46   And Jesus said, Somebody hath touched me: for I perceive that virtue is gone out of me.

47   And when the woman saw that she was not hid, she came trembling, and falling down before him, she declared unto him before all the people for what cause she had touched him, and how she was healed immediately.

48   And he said unto her, Daughter, be of good comfort: thy faith hath made thee whole; go in peace.

I love the song, "When Desperation Meets Faith" by the Pfeifers. While the song may be old, the message behind the song, will never grow old. The same message is found in the song "One Touch" by Nicole C. Mullen. The message found in both songs, and in the Word of God (Luke 8:43-48-KJV) refers to a woman who was in need of a touch.

The Bible tells of a woman who had been sick for many years, with an issue of blood. In an effort to be well, she did all she knew to do. She spent all of her money, time, and energy to be well, to be normal, and to be healed. Exhausted, frustrated and ready to give up, she heard that the Messiah was coming through her town. I can imagine she asked herself, "could it be? Could this be it for me? Could He really be a healer and I actually be healed?"

Something rose up in her for a yearning to be whole. There was a DESPERATION to just get near him. Believing if she could just touch him, things would be different. She was willing for just a small, quick, or maybe even a brush of him. She was willing to just touch the hem of his garment. She was willing to be vulnerable, maybe for the first time in her life. I pray you will go to your word and read about her miracle for yourself. I believe you will be blessed as many have been.

I want to share a couple of thoughts from this passage with you for you to consider:

She was sick and had been for many years. She was tired, she had done all she knew to do and she was desperate. She knew the Messiah was coming through her area and she was willing to do what she needed to do to get near to Him. Out of her DESPERATION AND FAITH, came not only her healing, but a knowledge of Who this Messiah was. He was her Jehovah Rapha, her Healer.

When desperation and faith collide, some great things will happen. The woman with the issue of blood found out for herself. She did not allow anything to stop her, not the crowds, the disciples, her shame, nor her humility. She pressed and pressed and pressed, until she could feel His garment in her hands.

When DESPERATION AND FAITH collide, Jehovah Rapha shows up, and heals. The woman with the issue of blood was made whole.

What is stopping you from your healing? Healing looks different for everyone. It may be a relationship, a medical condition, a thought, salvation, financial, etc. What is it that you need? Jehovah Rapha is coming through! Do not allow anything to block you from your touch; not pride, shame, humility, time, or faith. Christ said all we needed was the faith of a mustard seed. A mustard seed is small, it is not big at all.

Father, in the Name of Jesus I pray for each one who will read this quick devotion. I pray Father that he/she would not allow anyone or anything to hinder them from their touch.

Father, may they be DESPERATE for healing and may they have the FAITH to follow it through. Thank you Jehovah Rapha, my Healer.

Blessings.

Prayer to Heal Our Land

Father we thank you in the name of Jesus and we bless your holy name. Father God, I thank you that you that you are true to your word, that you cannot lie and great is your faithfulness. Father God, that if you say in the name of Yeshua, that you are going to do something, then Father God, you're gonna do it. If you make a promise, and when you make a promise Father God, you make good on those promises, and there are so many promises found, Lord God in the word. So, Father God, we release those promises upon the land right now Lord God, especially Father God, one promise that says, in 2 Chronicles 7:14, that if my people, who are called by my name shall humble themselves, shall seek my face, shall turn from their wicked ways, then I will hear from Heaven and I will heal their land.

Father God, I'm asking You in the name of Jesus, because I can, because I can come into Your presence very boldly on behalf of this land. Father God, I can come into Your presence very boldly on behalf of this world and that, Father God is exactly what I'm doing this morning. Father, I'm coming into Your presence very boldly. Father, I have asked You to search my heart, Father God You have searched me, You have searched my heart and You know me Lord God, like no one else knows me. You have pointed out the sin that is in me, You have pointed out, Father God, the things that I have done wrong, the hardness that I've had in my heart towards people. Father God, You have even given me the names of the people Lord God and I have repented before You and I have asked You to forgive me Father God.

I have taken, as an act of repentance, I have taken, Lord God, communion this morning, where I have trusted in the work of Your body Lord God on the cross, where I have trusted in the work of Your blood on the cross Father God, to save me, to heal me, to set me free and to give me an eternal home with you Lord God. I have trusted in those things this morning and because I have Lord God, and because I'm Yours and because I'm saved hallelujah, then You tell me that I can come into Your very presence boldly and because of the work of the cross Lord God, the veil was torn and I don't need to go to my pastor, I don't need to go to my priest, I don't need to go to somebody and then have them go to You, I can come boldly into Your presence. Father God, I speak 2 Chronicles 7:14 in your hearing, Father not that You need me to do it, because You said it and it's a done deal but because You allow me to do it.

Father, You said in 2 Chronicles, if my people, who are called by my name, shall humble themselves and seek my face, turn from their wicked ways, then I will hear from Heaven and I will heal their land. Father, I am your people, I belong to You Father God, I am a child of the King, so I am Yours. Father, You said to me if my people, who are called by my name, I am called, Father God by Your name.

I am called, Father God by Your name because I belong to You and You said if you will humble yourselves, Father God, I have humbled myself and will continue humbling myself Lord God Almighty before You and I have turned from my wicked ways, I have asked you to search me, You have searched me, I have repented of what You have shown me, I have turned from my wicked ways. I am seeking your face on a regular basis Lord God. You said if you would do these things, my people, then I will hear from Heaven and I will heal your land.

Father, I'm asking You in the name of Jesus, I'm asking you in the name of Jesus to heal our land, in Your name I pray, knowing with full confidence that You have heard me and that because I'm Yours, because I've humbled myself, because I've turned from my wicked ways, because I've repented, because I'm seeking Your face, then I have full confidence in the cross, in the word, in the tomb, in the resurrection, that You have heard me. Now Father, be faithful to Your word and to Your promises and to Your people. In Your name we pray, amen, amen, amen, and thank You, Lord.

The God Who Leads

Psalm 23 (KJV)

1 The Lord is my shepherd; I shall not want.

2 He maketh me to lie down in green pastures: he leadeth me beside the still waters.

3 He restoreth my soul: he leadeth me in the paths of righteousness for his name's sake.

4 Yea, though I walk through the valley of the shadow of death, I will fear no evil: for thou art with me; thy rod and thy staff they comfort me.

5 Thou preparest a table before me in the presence of mine enemies: thou anointest my head with oil; my cup runneth over.

6 Surely goodness and mercy shall follow me all the days of my life: and I will dwell in the house of the Lord forever.

...He leads me beside still waters... Psalm 23 (KJV)

I remember as a child playing "follow the leader" with my siblings. Being from a family of six children, and being the fifth born, it was highly unlikely that I would ever be the leader. Typically, my older brothers or sister served as the leader. As we played, they decided where we went and what we did.

We just simply followed, sometimes asking questions, complaining, or just refusing to follow any longer. This sounds a lot like God and His children down through the ages, doesn't it?

Since the beginning of time there has always been a leader. God the Father, Christ the Son and the Holy Spirit, known as the Trinity, have always been in the role of LEADER. Both the Old and New Testament give us many times where God, Jesus and the Holy Spirit led. God led Adam to the garden, and because he failed to listen, God led him out of the garden. God led the children of Israel and because they failed to listen it took them much longer to arrive in the promised land. God led his children to safety as he took them through the Red Sea, and eventually to the land he promised.

In the New Testament, Jesus led his disciples to himself as he revealed himself as The Way, The Truth, The Life. He led them to the gospel so they may be saved and lead others to salvation. He led the people who followed him to hope, healing, refreshment and service. Jesus led the people to Jerusalem and Calvary, where they watched their leader die a cruel and horrible death so they might live. He led them to the tomb, and much to their amazement, he was not there. One day he will lead them to his Father in Heaven for eternity.

God's leadership did not come without opposition. There were always those who followed and those who did not. Some accepted his leadership and there were others who said, "no way am I following this God, this man." Choosing not to follow came with a high price, yet, so does following.

What about you? Who has the place of leadership in your life? God has been a trusted Leader down through the ages and he will continue to do so into eternity. Will you allow Him to be the God Who leads in your life, your family, your heart, your home?

Father, I praise you as the God Who leads. Father, you have led your people since the beginning of time. Help me to be open and obedient to Your leading, in Jesus Name, Amen.

Blessings.

Prayer & Blessings Over Blane

Father in the name of Jesus, I bless Your Holy Name. Father, what a privilege it is to be a mother. What a privilege it is to be a mother who loves the Lord, not one who is perfect and certainly one who has made a lot of mistakes. Father, you know that if I could do a redo, man I would do so many things differently, but I cannot do that. But You have allowed me to be the mother to two amazing babies, boys, teenagers, young men, and husbands and with this oldest one, a father. So, Father, I count it a privilege to pray over my oldest son, Blane. I count it a privilege to pray a prayer of blessing over him. Father, it's my heart, that when I complete this and send it to him, Father God, that when he reads it, that the very anointing and favor of the Lord would rest upon him tenfold, Father God. I pray Lord God Almighty, that amazing things would happen to this young man as he reads this blessing, not because of me Father God, but because of how much you love him. Father, thank you for the opportunity to be Blane's mom.

Son, I want to tell you, you're an amazing young man and I am beyond proud of you. I am thankful for the young man that you have become, the father that you are, the husband that you are and that Blane Lee, man if you could only see, and maybe you have, I don't know, but my heart is that you would be able to see what I see in you, what Father has revealed to me of who you are. Man, if you could just see that, and you will, you will, and I know that you will. So, I want to tell you and my prayer is that you will receive It, that you will absolutely receive what I am getting ready to say to you.

There is a Paul in you that is waiting to come out. There is a Paul in you, that is waiting to come out! The Apostle Paul turned this world upside down for Jesus Christ and you will do the same thing. That is so why, and you've heard me say this and I think sometimes you just get tired of me saying it and it's okay, that's why the enemy is hot and heavy after you. That is why he is doing everything he can to stop you in your tracks. That's why he's fighting you in your marriage, that's why he's fighting you as a father, that's why he's fighting you in your health, that's why he's fighting you PERIOD. Because the enemy knows what is in you and he is scared to death to allow it to come forth.

So, Father, in the name of Jesus, I bless my oldest son. Father, I bless him Lord God Almighty that the days on Earth that he has Father God, will be prosperous Father, he will not want for one thing.

Father, I pray that his finances, Father God are straight and that he has an abundance and Father God, that there is not one thing that he needs that he does not have. I pray Father God, that every need will be supplied tenfold. I pray that he will prosper Lord God in his finances.

Father God, I pray a prayer of blessing over his health and I pray Father God that his heart is regulated, that his weight is gonna begin falling off Lord God Almighty. That the anxiety has been stilled, that he is no longer anxious Father God, he no longer worries, he is no longer fearful or afraid. I pray Father God, that his thoughts are in line with the word of God, that they are calm, and they are still and that they are so on you Father God. I pray that his mind is in order, that his mind is calm, and peace resides in his mind and his body.

Father God I pray for the spirit man of Blane and I pray Father God, that first of all, I want to ask Blane to forgive me for any harm that I have caused him in his walk as a young man of God. Father, that if there is anything that I have done to hinder him from following you, from hindering him from loving you and from hindering him from desiring you, I ask him to forgive me right now.

I pray over his spirit man Father God and I thank you in the name of Jesus that Blane Lee Jr. was committed to you long before he was born, that you knew him long before the foundations of the Earth and that you called him to be who you have called him to be. That even no matter how hard he may try to run from it, if in fact that's what he's doing, I don't know Father, you know, that he will settle in his spirit that you have called him out and you have called him for a purpose and you have called him for a destiny and he will walk in that purpose, in that calling and in that destiny.

Father, I pray a prayer over his marriage in the name of Jesus, I pray that he would love his wife the way that you love the church and I pray that he would draw himself to his wife Father God, and she would draw herself to him Father God, that you would give them an absolute amazing marriage and they would return to each other, they would return to the vows that they both made years ago in August and that they would surrender their marriage and themselves to you, Father God.

I pray for Blane Lee and a prayer of blessing over Blane as a father. Father, you have given this young man two beautiful, amazing, smart girls, smart daughters Lord God and I pray that Blane Lee would show those girls how much he loves them, that he would show them what it means to be loved and that they would always find their love in their daddy and in Father

God and that they would never, ever, ever go look for love that should come from their daddy in a man Father God.

So, I pray over my oldest son, I pray that he would prosper in his job Lord God at Archer Lodge. I pray Father God, that Blane Lee would prosper, he would advance, and he would be promoted, Father God. I pray Father, that because you're gonna cause his finances to prosper, that he's gonna be able to let go of one of those jobs and he's gonna be able to spend more time with his family. I pray Father God, that he would have a yearning to be at home with his wife and his daughters more than he does anything else. I thank you Father God that you're gonna cause this family to be absolutely amazing, drawn to you and they will be a model family Father God and you would use them Father God to bless other families and show them how to love and care for each other and care for Father.

Father, the day you blessed me with this young man has been a most amazing day in my life and I don't know that I've always told him that, I don't know that he has always felt that, but Father I am beyond proud and blessed to be his mother. So, Father God, in this blessing, I pray that he hears exactly what it is that you want him to hear and may his life be completely changed. I pray that the very favor of the Lord rests upon you Blane, a thousand-fold and I pray this in the name of Jesus, because he told me I could, and I call it done. Hallelujah, hallelujah, hallelujah, and we bless you Father, we praise you Father and I bless my son Blane, Amen.

In Step with the Master
Matthew 16:24 (ESV)

Then Jesus told his disciples, "If anyone would come after me, let him deny himself and take up his cross and follow me.

Over the course of years, I have watched Bruzer, my husband's dog and four legged best friend, follow Roger everywhere. As Roger stepped, Bruzer stepped. As Roger stopped, Bruzer stopped. Bruzer always positioned himself to see his Master, no matter where he was. There were many times that Bruzer would follow Roger to work in the fields. Bruzer would position himself at every row to see and keep an eye on his Master. If possible, as distance would allow it, Roger was never out of Bruzer's site. As I watched the two of them together, moving and stopping in sync, the Lord reminded me that this is a picture of He and His children, this is His heart for His followers. Father God's desire is that His followers come to know him passionately, personally and purposefully, just like Bruzer knows Roger. This type of knowing only comes through deep and devoted connection and time, which leads to following.

To call one master is to believe and trust in that person that you are willing to follow them wherever they lead. It takes a trust unlike any other that requires a surrender of oneself to the one you are following, much like Bruzer and Roger. Being a follower of Father God, as your Master, begins with a desire to know Him personally, purposefully and passionately. What about you? Are you a follower of Father God and is He your Master? Today is a beautiful day to make that decision. Maybe you have been a follower in the past, yet, you feel the burden is too heavy so you stopped. Today, choose to recommit your walk to Father.

Father God, I am so thankful that you are trustworthy and worth following. Father help us to follow You completely as we commit our entire beings to you. You are the Great and Merciful Master and worthy of following.

Blessings.

Prayer & Blessings Over Jonathon

Father, I thank You in the name of Jesus for my youngest son, Jonathon, and Father, You've given me the opportunity to pray a prayer of blessing over him and I thank You for this moment. Father, I thank You that You chose me to be Jonathon's mom and Father, I thank You for the young man that he has become. Father, I pray over him right now and I pray Father God that Jonathon would always know how much I love him. Father, I pray that any harm that I have caused in my youngest son Jonathon, that he would forgive me for that harm right now in the name of Jesus.

Father God, I pray that even before I get ready to bless him, that he would receive the words that I am getting ready to speak over him and I pray Father God, that he would receive them straight from the throne of God. I pray that he would not hear me Father God, but he would hear you. I pray that he would see these words as truth, he would receive this blessing Lord God and he would walk in the absolute favor of you Father God in the name of Jesus.

So, Jonathon, I thank you that you are mine. I thank you that you are my son, I am beyond proud of you, that God would choose me to be your momma, is amazing. That God would give me such an amazing young man who is tender hearted and compassionate and loving to others blows me out of the water. That even in the midst of many struggles that you and I have had, Jonathon, as you have become a young man, your heart has always been tender to me and I thank you for that. I thank you so much for the young man you are, for the young man that Father has called you to be.

I thank you for the husband that you are to your wife and the Father that you are going to be to the children that Father God will give you. I thank you that you love the Lord with all your heart, and I am beyond excited, Jonathon to see what God is up to in you. You know that God's hand is on your life, you know that his anointing is on your life and you know already Jonathon, that Father has called you to the nations.

I pray that you would never lose sight of what Father has called you to do. I pray that you would know it and understand it for yourself. That you would not just receive it from other people, but that you would know it in your heart. I pray Jonathon, that you would not be so caught up with material things that you would miss what God has done and what God is doing in your life. I pray that your heart is always tender. I pray that the scripture that you sent me years ago, in the book of Luke would become YOUR scripture and you would speak it over you, you would pray it over you on a regular basis.

I see you as a Timothy from the word of God, a young Timothy and I pray that you would find for yourself a Paul and maybe God has even given you a Paul even in name, maybe you've just not connected your heart with this Paul and gone in covenant with this Paul, but I pray that you would know who God has called you to be.

Jonathon, this is the word that Father gave me this week and your daddy prayed it over me, it's found in 2 Timothy 1:6, it's where Paul, the Apostle Paul was telling young Timothy fan into flame the gift that God has put in you. The Apostle Paul is saying when I laid hands on you, and Jonathon, God has gifted you like crazy. I am just going to give you that word right now where Paul is telling Timothy fan into flame. Because, what we know is that sometimes a flame can get low, yet when we fan that flame it gets higher and higher and higher and it gets bigger and bigger and bigger. So, I am praying over you just as Paul prayed over Timothy, that you will fan into flame the spiritual gift that God has put in you. Son, as I pray this prayer of blessing over you, I pray that you would receive it.

Father, in the name of Jesus, I bless my youngest son Jonathon Brooks Lee. Father, I bless him first and foremost in his spiritual being, I pray and bless him Lord God that he would know that he knows who You are as his personal Lord and Savior and that he would understand and know the call that is on his life. I bless him Lord God, that not only would he know the call, but he would know the giftedness and that he would begin walking in his giftedness. I bless him Lord God, that the Paul that you have appointed and anointed for him is there and I pray that as I'm blessing him right now, that you're even bringing the name of the Paul to him.

I bless him Lord God in his work, that everything that his hands do and every place that his feet trod would be holy ground. I pray that he would understand the power in a touch, and I pray and bless him Lord God with anointed hands, that his hands are so anointed Father God, that when he puts his hands on people, that the Holy Spirit would immediately convict them and that whatever they need to do or stop doing, they would have to do it in the name of Jesus. I pray Father God, that his body is well and strong and that his physical being Lord God, is in perfect alignment and attunement with you Father God. I bless him Lord God, that his heart is pure and holy, and that forgiveness always rules and reigns in his heart. That he is compassionate as you are compassionate. I pray Father God that his emotional being is aligned with you Father, his mind is still, and his mind is settled, and it is in good perfect peace, that his heart Lord God is perfect Father God. That his body from head to toe is well and in good health

Father God. That his eyes always see your beauty, his ears are always discerning and hearing what thus saith the Lord thy God and that his discernment, his discernment Father God is intensified a thousand-fold. I pray Father God that his prophetic eyes and ears are in tune with yours Lord God Almighty and that he would speak truth in the name of Jesus. I pray that his finances Lord God Almighty would not go lacking. Father God, I pray that because you own all the cattle on a thousand hills, that you would bless him with above and beyond all the finances that he needs. I pray Father God, that his finances are so in order, a thousand-fold Father God and that he has everything he needs and that you are blessing him even right now beyond even his needs, and you are blessing him with his wants. I pray over his marriage, like crazy, that you would draw the two of them together, that they would be such an example for other couples. Father, I pray that you would draw him closer to you. I pray that he would hunger and thirst after righteousness because he will be filled. I pray this blessing over him Father. God, I pray that as he reads it and receives it, it is as if it is coming out of your own lips Father. I pray Father God, that he would pass on a blessing to his wife, and he would pass on a blessing to the children that you have in his quiver that are to come. Father, I thank you for Jonathon, I thank you for allowing me to be his mother and what a blessing. May I always be a mother that points him to Jesus Christ and speaks truth to him and always takes him back to the word of God. Son, in the name of Jesus, I bless you with all the blessing that is given me from the throne of God. Blessing and honor belong to you son, in the name of Jesus, Amen.

From Boredom to Boldness

Psalm 46:10 (AMP)

"Be still and know (recognize, understand) that I am God. I will be exalted among the nations! I will be exalted in the earth."

Our world has come to a halt. Life as we have known it changed drastically around March 13, 2020. A pandemic hit this world from one end to the other almost shutting down everything. People were deemed either essential or non-essential. Those deemed as essential, could continue their work as required. Those not deemed essential were required to follow "stay at home orders." People were bored, restless, and wondering how long this would last. The entire time, Father is causing all things to work together for His good. Out of boredom came a boldness among the people. People finally had all the time they needed, there were no more excuses. People, for the first time had to be "Still." The stillness brought about a boldness in homes, families, couples, individuals, and children. Those who did not have time to play instruments any longer, started playing and sharing. Those told to write, finally started writing, and those who have put off projects were now completing various projects around their home. Couples who spent a lot of time working now had time for each other and made some lasting changes in their relationships. Parents who did not previously have time to just play and enjoy their kids are now their kid's teachers and are with them 24 hours a day, with plenty of time to play. The Psalmist said In Psalm 46:10, "Be still and know (recognize, understand) that I am God. I will be exalted among the nations! I will be exalted in the earth." People all over this world have been still, and slowed down.

From this stillness has come a boldness from writers, singers, instrumentalists, teachers, preachers and many more. God has been exalted through the boldness that has come from the stillness of the land, just as He said.

Father, thank you that your Word is true and will go forth regardless of what is going on. Thank you, Father, for allowing good to come from this stillness as well as the boldness that has come forth from your people. May this boldness continue even as the stillness changes. Amen.

Blessings.

Prayer for Jesus, Neci, & Luke

So, this is really amazing that today on February the 4th, a little before 7 o'clock in reading the book of Luke, which is where the Lord has taken me, in chapter 4, so I'm reading as Jesus enters into the synagogue. He had just been taken to the wilderness and tempted by Satan. So, the word of God says that then Satan had to leave Him, but he left Him just for a season. So then, Jesus makes His way into Galilee and then He makes His way into Nazareth, which is really His home, and picking up in verse 16, it says that when Jesus arrived into Nazareth, He went into the synagogue. One of the neat things about Jesus is that during His ministry, Jesus was always finding His way into the synagogue, into the temple.

So, it says that He went into the synagogue, it was the Sabbath day, and He stood up to read and there was delivered unto Him, this is verse 17, the book of the prophet Isaiah, and when He had opened the book, He found the place where it was written. Verse 18, and this is what I believe the Lord is giving me for this day, the spirit of the Lord is upon me, because He has anointed me to preach the gospel to the poor. He has sent me to heal the broken hearted, to preach deliverance to the captives and recovering of sight to the blind, to set at liberty them that are bruised. Verse 19 goes on to say, and to preach the acceptable year of the Lord, and I love the fact that in verse 20, it says, and this reading is from the King James version, it says and He closed the book and He gave it again to the minister and Jesus sat down and it says that all of the eyes of the people were fastened upon Him in the synagogue that day. But after He read the word, because He is the Word, He closed the book and He sat down, because He was finished. The word of God will speak for itself in the ears of the hearer. The word of God will preach itself in the ears of the hearer, and I love that word because I believe that's what the Lord has called me to do.

The book of Isaiah 61:1-2, which is exactly what Luke, Doctor Luke was speaking, says the spirit of the Lord is upon me. I'm gonna make this personal, because I believe this is what the Lord is saying to me right now. Neci, the spirit of the Lord is upon you, because He has anointed you to preach the gospel to the poor. He has sent you to heal the broken hearted, to preach deliverance to the captives, those who are in chains and bondage, and recovery of sight to the blind. To set free those that are bruised and to preach the acceptable year of the Lord. {Singing} Lord, prepare me to be a sanctuary that's pure and holy, it's tried and it's true with thanksgiving, I will be a living sanctuary for you.

See, there's a little bit of rumbling going on that started last night and I allowed myself, maybe to be connected to that rumbling. So, I'm asking the Lord this morning as I'm in my quiet time, I said "Father, if this were You, if You were sitting where I'm sitting right now, and this rumbling is trying to happen... because what we know about Jesus, is that His entire ministry was about rumblings because the Pharisees and the Sadducees hated Him, because of the word that was IN HIM, and THEY HATED HIM. So, I said, "Jesus, if you were sitting here in my place, with this little bit of rumbling, what would You do? How would You handle it?" So clearly, I heard Jesus say to me, "Neci, I would get up from among it and I would be about my Father's business, because that's all that matters."

So, this morning, I choose to be about my Father's business because that's all that matters. Father clearly said to me, that "Neci, I need you to hear this morning, that Luke 4:18 is for you, that the spirit of the Lord is upon you Neci, because he has anointed you to preach the gospel to the poor. He hath sent you to heal the brokenhearted, He has sent you to preach deliverance to the captives and recovering of sight to the blind. To set at liberty them that are bruised. Neci, He has sent you to preach the acceptable year of the Lord, so the rumblings are going to come, the rumblings are always going to be there, but will YOU choose this day and every moment forward, will you choose Neci, to be about your Father's business? Will you choose to get up from among the rumblings and not even allow the rumblings to bother you, to hinder you? Would you get up from among them and be about your Father's business?"

So, I want to answer, because I think that's a question that you posed to me Father and I want to answer it in word, and I want to answer it in song. So, I want to say to you yes, Jesus! I heard you and I will obey your voice and I will get up from among the rumblings and I will be about my Father's business. I want to ask you this morning as I sing in praise to you, that you truly would prepare me to be a sanctuary that is pure, that is holy, that is tried and true.

{singing}
Lord prepare me to be a sanctuary that's pure and holy, it's tried and it's true
With thanksgiving, I'll be a living sanctuary for you Lord prepare me to be a sanctuary that's pure and holy, it's tried and it's true with thanksgiving, I'll be a living sanctuary for you Father, that's my prayer to You this morning, and my praise, would You receive it, and would it be like sweet incense to You and would You inhabit that praise in the name of Jesus, amen.

Small Seed, BIG MOVES
Matthew 17:20 KJV

And Jesus said unto them, Because of your unbelief: for verily I say unto you, If ye have faith as a grain of mustard seed, ye shall say unto this mountain, Remove hence to yonder place; and it shall remove; and nothing shall be impossible unto you.

I wonder if you remember a time in your life, when you were not chosen for a team because you were too small. Maybe, you were not invited by the older kids to go to the movies or skating because you were too small. Or, while all the older kids could ride the cool rides at the amusement park you had to just simply watch, because you were too small.

Being small while growing up was not always a good thing. The word small carried more of a negative connotation than a positive. Oftentimes smaller children were overlooked more than their counterparts and maybe always told, "you are too small."

Yet, small, from a biblical perspective takes on a whole new meaning. David was a small shepherd boy who not only killed Goliath, but did so with a small stone and a sling. King Josiah was a small 8 years old when he took the throne. Jesus encouraged the small children to come to him. The small mustard seed, carried in it, big moves.

Jesus told his disciples in the Book of Matthew that if they had faith as small as a mustard seed, they could say to a mountain to move and it would move. Such a small seed for such a big move.

What about you? Is there a big move in your life that needs a mustard seed faith? A mustard seed of faith is a MUST for big moves.

Father, thank you for the smallness of the mustard seed. I am thankful that such a small faith can result in major moves. Father, help me when my seed cannot even be seen, due to unbelief. In Jesus Name, Amen.

Blessings.

Prayer for Parents & Children

Father God, in the name of Jesus we bless You. Father, we thank You and we praise You that You are our Father, that You are our Lord, You are our protector, and Savior. In You, Father God, resides the Trinity, the Father, the Son and the Holy Spirit. Father, I thank You in the name of Jesus that in You, You teach us how to be parents and how to love. In You Father, You teach us how to be children and love our parents.

Father, I thank You for parents and I thank You for children. Father God, I'm thankful that in the book of Psalms 127, You say to us; Except the Lord build the house, they labor in vain that build it. Except the Lord keep the city, the watchmen waketh, but in vain. Verse 2, it is vain for you to rise up early, to sit up late, to eat the bread of sorrows for so he giveth his beloved sleep. Verse 3, Lo, children are a heritage from the Lord and the fruit of the womb is his reward. Verse 4, As arrows are in the hand of a mighty man, so are children of one's youth. Verse 5, Happy is the man who has his quiver full of them, they shall not be ashamed, but they shall speak with the enemies at the gate. Father, I thank You that you allow husband and wife to come together, to procreate children.

Children have always been important to you God, and You showed this many times in the Bible, including in the New Testament, Lord God, where Jesus said to his disciples, do not hinder these little ones from coming to me, for such is the Kingdom. I thank You for children, I thank you Lord God Almighty that you love children and you have always loved them. Because You love children, You love their parents Lord God, who join You in creation, in bringing forth children. Father, I pray that children would ALWAYS be a blessing to their parents. Father God, I know sometimes parents get frustrated, they get overwhelmed and they get overworked

Lord God, and instead of children being a blessing to them, they're a hinderance to them.

Father God, I pray in the name of Jesus that from this day forward, that would not be so. That from this day forward Lord God Almighty, parents would see their children as a blessing from Jesus Christ and God the Father. I pray that they would not become so overwhelmed and so worn and so tired Lord God, that they would not cause their hand to be raised against their children, that they would not cause their children to be sent away from them Lord God, that they would not harm their children. But I pray, Father God, that just as You have patience with us, that we as parents would have patience with our children and with our grandchildren.

I pray, Father God, that we would always set aside time to spend with our children getting to know them and feeding into their lives and speaking into their lives Lord God. I thank you Father God, that in the book of Deuteronomy Chapter 6, Lord God, you say the following; 1, Now these are the commandments, the statutes, and the ordinances which the Lord, your God commanded to teach you, that you might do them in the land to which you go to possess it: 2, That thou might fear the Lord thy God, to keep all of his statutes and his commandments, which I command thee, thou, and thy son, and thy son's son, all of the days of the life; and thy days may be prolonged. 3, Hear therefore, oh Israel, and observe to do it; that it may be well with thee, and that ye may increase mightily, as the Lord God of thy fathers hath promised thee, in the land that floweth with milk and honey. 4, Hear, oh Israel, the Lord our God is one Lord: 5, And thou shalt love the Lord thy God with ALL of thine heart, and with all of thy soul, and with all of thy might. 6, And these words, which I command thee this day, shall be in thine heart: 7, And thou shalt teach them diligently unto thy children, and shalt talk of them when thou sittest in thine house, and when thou walkest by the way, and when thy liest down, and when thou risest up. 8, And thou shalt bind them for a sign upon thine hand, and they shall be as frontlets between thine eyes.

Father, I thank You that You have commanded us to teach the children. That You have commanded us to spend time with the children Lord God. You tell us, Father God, in Psalms 139:13-14, For thou has possessed my reins: thou hast covered me in my mother's womb. I will praise thee; for I am fearfully and wonderfully made; marvelous are thy works; and that my soul knoweth right well. In 2 Timothy 3:14-15 you tell us, but continue thou in the things which thou hast learned and has been assured of, knowing of whom thou hast learned them; And that from a child thou hast known the holy scriptures, which are able to make thee wise unto salvation through faith which is in Christ Jesus.

So, Father God, I thank You for parents, I thank You for children. I pray Father God that as parents we would take our lead from you and I pray Father God, that as children we would respect our parents so that our days on Earth may be longer. As we begin and continue building the lives of our children, just as You instructed us to do Father, I pray as parents and as grandparents that we would build character into our children and our grandchildren. Not only would we build character, Lord God, but we would walk it out ourselves. I pray Father God, that we would build and walk out patience, faithfulness, self-control, truthfulness, goodness, wisdom, virtue, gentleness, humility, serving, kindness, compassion, obedience, faithfulness, a teachable spirit, contentment, responsibility, endurance, discernment, and generosity. Father, You have been the greatest example for all of us and may we as parents, grandparents and children, may we walk out the example that You have left for us, that You have shown us, that You have spoken over us and may we not grow weary Lord in doing well.

So, Father, as we pray over our parents, grandparents and our children, we pray a prayer of blessing. Greater than anything, may we always love you with our entire being, as we love you, Father God may we be an example to others of what love, unconditional love looks like, in the name of Jesus, Amen.

Sifting is Necessary
Luke 22:31-32 (KJV)

"And the Lord said, Simon, Simon, behold, Satan hath desired to have you, that he may sift you as wheat; But I have prayed for thee, that thy faith fail not. And when thou art converted, strengthen thy brethren."

Sifting, according to Merriam-Webster, is "to go through (something) very carefully in order to find something useful or valuable. Sifting can happen on several different levels and many different ways. We sift flour before baking, farmers sift wheat to separate the wheat and chaff and miners sift sand looking for stones, and rare jewels. In each case, the sifting that is happening is for good in an effort to find the best and valuable of what is being sifted. Peter was a lover and disciple of Jesus. In order for him to be his best for the gospel's sake; Jesus allowed Satan to sift him as wheat. Satan thought Peter could not survive the sifting; however, Jesus was praying for Peter, and Jesus knew better. Sifting Peter as wheat meant that what was in his very core, who he really was, would come forth. Satan had no clue that this sifting would make Peter a better man, disciple and lover of the Messiah. Jesus said to Peter, when the sifting is over and you are converted, strengthen thy brothers. Peter, converted and strengthened after the sifting, did just that. Peter was the one who stood up at Pentecost, preached the Word and thousands were saved. Sifting was necessary for Peter to be the man Jesus needed him to be. What about you, are you open to the sifting of the Holy Spirit? Are you willing to see who you really are at your core? Are you willing to be used by Father, to carry the gospel and strengthen the brethren? Father, may we desire to be sifted as wheat so that the best and valuable of us may come forth. Father help us to love and desire you more than remaining the same. Father, sift us as wheat and then help us to strengthen the brethren. Amen.

41

Blessings.

Let The Babes Come
Luke 18:15-17 (NLT)

15   One day some parents brought their little children to Jesus so he could touch and bless them. But when the disciples saw this, they scolded the parents for bothering him.

16   Then Jesus called for the children and said to the disciples, "Let the children come to me. Don't stop them! For the Kingdom of God belongs to those who are like these children.

17   I tell you the truth, anyone who doesn't receive the Kingdom of God like a child will never enter it."

Children are a gift from the Lord and have always been important to Him and His creation. They were created and formed with a natural bent, which basically means who God created them to be. Jesus understood the importance of children and their place in the kingdom. He knew their example of faith should always be followed by adults. The disciples did not clearly understand Jesus' care and love for children and needed to be taught. Jesus stopped, rebuked, and taught them the importance of children, faith, and the kingdom.

As parents it is our responsibility to join God in the forming and growing of the child's natural bent. When we fail to learn and understand the love Jesus has for children, and the child's natural bent, we are doing a disservice to the child, the kingdom, and their future. Seeing children from the same lens as Jesus sees them, loving them and growing them up in who they were created to be is 'letting the babes come.'

How about you, are you letting the babes come? Are you helping them to grow into the natural bent given them by God before they were formed in mom's womb?

Father, thank You for the children you have given us, whether through birth or by gift. Help us to see these children through your lens and not our own. Help us to see and understand who You have created them to be so we can partner with You in growing them into their natural bent. Help us, Father, to let the babes come. Amen.

Blessings.

Prayer Over Testing

Father, in the name of Jesus we come before You, blessing and honoring You. Saying yes and amen to You, surrendering to You everything that You put into us long before the foundations of the Earth. Father, You are THE God, who knows all things, You are THE God, Who is all knowing, all knowledgeable. You are THE God, Who long before the foundations of the Earth, was, and currently You are, and in the future, You will be, because You're a God that stands the test of time.

Father, I am so thankful that all wisdom and all knowledge is held in Your hand. You tell us your people, if any man lack wisdom let him ask, because You give graciously, You give generously, You give goodly. You tell us in Your word Father, that we have not because we ask not. So, Father, I'm asking you right now in the name of Jesus, on behalf of this precious young woman and this precious family Father God, that You ordained long before, long before, Father God, the foundations of the Earth.

Father, the enemy is fighting so hard to tear them apart, the enemy is fighting so hard to destroy them. The enemy is fighting so hard for their marriage to be desolate, but praise God and hallelujah, that the battle has already be won, the victory is won, it was won on the cross. So, Father God, I pray over them, I pray over their marriage and Father, this morning I especially pray over the wisdom and knowledge that You are granting this young woman right now.

So, Father, we ask You to give her total recall of everything she's studied, everything that she has prepared for and Father we thank You in the name of Jesus that You have already hand selected the seat or the computer that she will be sitting at, I'm not sure how her test will go, but you already know. Father, I pray and thank you in advance that the Holy Spirit is already resting in that place, that the peace that passes all understanding is already resting in that place. So, Father God, I pray that she would go with the confidence that comes from Jesus Christ alone. I pray Father God, that she would reach deep to get the confidence that comes in Jesus Christ alone and I pray Father God, that she would not be fearful, that she would not be anxious, that she would not be worried, that she would trust you Father God.

I pray that as she sits to take her test, Lord God, I pray that she would breathe, that she would take a moment, she would surrender this test to you, the outcome to you and Father God, I pray that you would give her total recall.

I pray in the name of Jesus Christ because You allow me to do so. I pray that when she reads the question, that You would give her clarity, that You would give her understanding. Father God, that she would immediately be able to find the answer and that she would know that she knows that she knows, that that is the answer to that question. Then I pray Father God, that she would not tarry, that she would not worry, that she would click appropriately if its computer based or circle, whatever the case may be and then she would move on.

I pray Father God, when all is said and done that everything, she needs to pass this test is in her and that she would understand that. I pray Father God, if this is the same test that she's taken before and not passed, that she would not give that another thought, when she goes in for this test, it would be like if she is taking it for the first time. I pray that fear would not grip her, fear would not rule, fear would not reign. As a matter of fact, I'm asking You right now, Father God, in Your word You say in 2 Timothy that You've not given us the spirit of fear but of power, of love and a sound mind. So, I pray in the name of Jesus, that You would saturate her with power of love and of a sound mind. I pray Lord God, that You would saturate her like crazy. So, Father, I pray that she would go forth in Your confidence and not in her own. Father, we are asking you for a positive outcome, we are asking You Father God that she would pass that test and that she would blow it out of the water, that it would be so amazing.

Father, in Your name we pray, we thank You, we bless You, we honor You. Amen.

The God Who FORGIVES

Matthew 26:8 (KJV)

But when his disciples saw it, they had indignation, saying, To what purpose is this waste?

John 3:16 (KJV)
16 For God so loved the world, that he gave his only begotten Son, that whosoever believeth in him should not perish, but have everlasting life.

Romans 10:9-10 (KJV)
9 That if thou shalt confess with thy mouth the Lord Jesus, and shalt believe in thine heart that God hath raised him from the dead, thou shalt be saved. 10 For with the heart man believeth unto righteousness; and with the mouth confession is made unto salvation.

The Attributes of God speak to His character, Who He is, and will always describe Him perfectly. He can never be less or operate contrary to Who He is.

As we enter into the Easter Season what better attribute of God to focus and meditate on, than the God who forgives. God's forgiveness is available and freely given to every person who asks and is willing to receive it. To forgive is to cancel, as in a debt. Forgiveness is a free gift. When God forgives us, He cancels, or does away with our debt/sin.

God's forgiveness has always been associated with blood, and is seen as a replacement for a person's sin. In the Old Testament, it was the blood of animals, which was offered by the Priest, once a year for the sins of the people. In the New

Testament, it was the blood of the spotless Lamb (Matthew 26:28), Jesus Christ. The blood was shed and offered for our sins (one time, once and for all) on the Cross, at Calvary. Jesus Christ, as the perfect man, is the only one who could offer the once and for all sacrifice. This sacrifice was a gift of Love from Father God as seen in John 3:16, for the forgiveness of our sins past, present and future.

That is what this Easter Season is all about, the forgiveness of sins, and the death, burial and resurrection of Jesus Christ. Because He came, loved, died and rose, you can be saved from eternal hell, and live with Christ for eternity.

Father, thank you for Your love towards us that You would send Jesus, the spotless Lamb to take our place, and bear our sins, on the cross. Thank you for the free gift of forgiveness and salvation. Your Word tells us in Romans 10:9-10, that, "if we confess with our mouth the Lord Jesus Christ and believe in our hearts that God raised Him from the dead, we SHALL BE SAVED." Father save your people. In Jesus Name, Amen.

Blessings.

Prayer Over Marriages

Heavenly Father I bless Your name; Father I bless Your holy name. Father I thank You and I praise You that You are a God of reconciliation. That You are a God of resurrection. That You are a God of restoration. That You are a God who LOVES Your people. Father I thank You in the name of Jesus that You are THE GOD and the ONLY GOD who instituted marriage. Father, I'm so thankful that You love marriage and that You care about marriage and that You care about couples Father God. That long before the foundations of the Earth, Father, You knew that there would be relationships, because You were in relationship Father, with the Son and with the Holy Spirit.

Father, relationships have been important to You for a long time, long before the foundations of the Earth. Father, You tell us in the book of Genesis, which we know as being like the first part of everything, that long before there was anything, there was You and the Son and the Holy Spirit, which indicates that long before there was anything, there was connection and there was relationship. There was not separateness and there was not isolation Father, because You and the Son and the Holy Spirit worked together in unison.

Father, I thank You for making the decision Father, for Adam, that Adam didn't need to be by himself, but that Adam needed a helper, he needed a helpmate. You saw, Father God that he didn't need to be alone because even the animals had somebody. So, Father, You caused a sleep to come upon him and You took a part of him, You took a rib, and from that rib, Father, You made woman. Father, just as You breathed life into Adam, You breathed life into his helper and then You placed her with him, and then You placed them in the garden. A place of beauty, a place of sanctuary, a place of goodness and perfectness. While it was not Your heart Father, that sin would enter into Adam and Eve, because You're a God of freewill, You didn't stop it and it changed the course of everything Father, which allowed for Jesus Christ to come to Earth as a man, because we needed a Savior.

Father, I thank You that You loved man enough that you brought woman. Father, Adam said in the garden, when he was awakened out of his deep sleep, he said she is BONE of MY BONE and she is FLESH of MY FLESH, she shall be called WOMAN. Father, a oneness, a ONENESS happened that day, so Father I pray in the name of Jesus over marriages, that a ONENESS would happen again. Father, that couples would understand that because of what happened in that garden, because of... and I say the garden, but because of what happened that DAY Father, when you caused Adam to be in a deep sleep and You TOOK from him, You took a part of him and You made woman, that they became ONE and that oneness has not changed and it can't change Father, yet we fight against it.

Granted, Father, we are individuals, we come into relationship and we come into marriage as separate individuals and when we make that covenant Father God, with YOU first and foremost and then with our partners, Father God, that separateness also brings about a oneness. So, Father, I pray that we would come back to a place of covenant with You Lord God, and then with each other. I pray Father God, that we would come to a place of oneness and that we would just stop and we would breathe and in breathing we would be reminded of the love that Jesus Christ has for us all the way to the cross, and that same love, he has asked us to have for our spouse.

So, Father, I pray a prayer of remembrance over marriages, that we would remember what You've done for us and that we would do the same for our spouse. I pray a prayer of grace over our marriages. I pray a prayer of mercy over our marriages and that we would be reminded that just as you have been merciful and gracious to us, that we would be merciful and gracious to our spouses. Father, I pray that You would cause us to settle and breathe and be reminded of Your love for us and how You tell us in Your word, now go and love others. So, I pray Father, that You would help us to LOVE OUR SPOUSES the way that You have loved us.

Father, I pray for restoration, reconciliation and resurrection in our marriages. I pray for a healing in our marriages and I pray that we would say Father, heal my heart, heal my spirit, heal my mind and when I look upon my spouse, may I see You and may I see the love that you have for me and allow me to extend that love to my partner. Father, where marriages are hurting, I pray that You would heal them, where marriages seem like they have just been buried Father, I pray that You would resurrect them and when marriages seem like they are distant, that they're just separate and separating, I pray that You would reconcile them. Father, I thank You that you're a God of redemption and You can redeem the time, You can redeem the love and You can redeem our marriages. So I ask You now, in the name of Jesus Christ, with all power and all authority that has been given to me because I am saved and set apart by Jesus Christ and I am co-heirs with Jesus, I pray that You would heal our marriages and I call it done in the name of Jesus, because You tell me that I can do so. Father, I pray a prayer of blessing over EVERY marriage in the name of Jesus. Amen.

It's a Ripple Effect
Acts 1:8 (KJV)

But you shall receive power, after the Holy Ghost is come upon you: and ye shall be witnesses unto me both in Jerusalem, and in all Judea, and in Samaria, and unto the uttermost part of the earth.

This thought of a ripple effect has been on my mind and heart for years. I use it when I talk with people both professionally and personally. As I think about a ripple effect, my minds turns to a pond, when a rock has been skipped (of course I could never skip rocks no matter how I tried) into the pond and it begins rippling from the point of entry. I see this point of entry as me, or a person I am talking to or about. From that point of entry, the ripple begins, creating a ripple with rings of full circles. The ripples continue for a distance until it is no longer and just simply fades. The greater the impact of the rock and water, the greater and longer the ripple last.

The rock, figuratively speaking, can be anything. It can be something good, such as love. Or it can be the opposite, it can be hate. It can be salvation or it can be choosing to do life my own way. The rock can represent a healthy relationship or an unhealthy one. Regardless of what the rock represents, it has an effect that will ripple. When it ripples, others are affected as well. The ripple closest to the impact, or person, is affected the most, and then the next, and the next, and so on and so on. A ripple effect can also be generational, as with each ripple a person is affected and so on and so on. If you consider this point of impact being you, how are you effecting others' lives? We are always making an impact on others, in a positive or negative way. As we effect those closest to us they are effecting others as well. My ripple today is affecting my grandchildren, their grandchildren and their grandchildren. What does your impact look like?

Father, I pray that you would help us to be mindful of our ripple and the impact it has on others. Help us to count the cost and initiate some major life changes for positive impact on those who we effect and those who will come after us. In Your Name I pray, Amen.

Blessings.

Prayer for Presence in the Storms

Father in the name of Jesus, Yeshua, the One who is more than able to accomplish what concerns us. The one who is more than able to walk along side of us. When life seems so heavy, when life just does not seem fair, when life throws us a curveball. When we just don't know what to do or where to turn, or who to turn to, Father I'm thankful in the name of Jesus, that You are a very present help in time of trouble, that You are our solid foundation when everything else around us seems to be shifting.

Father, even the weather is so unpredictable and right now, Father God, we are in a time of weather where we are watching hurricane Dorian. But what's so beautiful, Father God, even in the midst of the storm, is that You are our peace. You are the storm calmer, You are the One who calms the storm, You are the One who speaks "peace, be still" in the midst of the storm. Father storms come to us, storms come to us in many ways. Father, it can be a loss of a friendship, it can be a loss of a family member, it can be a loss of a job, it can be a loss of girlfriends or boyfriends. Father God, it can just be a loss Father, but loss is loss, no matter what form it takes, no matter which way it comes, no matter how it comes, loss is loss.

Father, I thank You that in the middle of loss, You are present. That not one thing Father God, that we lose catches You by surprise, but because You are always present, all powerful and all knowing, Father God, any loss we suffer, any loss we celebrate comes through your hands first. While we do not understand it Father, that is what faith is all about and that is what trust is all about. So, Father, I pray that You would help us when we just do not get it. I pray that You would help us Father, when the losses come and they catch us by surprise, or maybe we have known the loss was gonna happen all along. Father, I pray that You would always be our solid foundation, You would always be the One that we come running to Father God, when things are just painful, when they're hard, when we don't understand.

I am thankful Father God that You understand all things, You know all things and You are always in all places. So, Father God, while You are right here with me during this time, You're also with my dear friend on the other side of the world in Belgium, and You're the next state over Father God for those that are there. You are across the waters, both Pacific and Atlantic. You are in different time zones, yet very present.

So, Father, I thank you for the truth that is wrapped up in the word, that You are a very present help in time of trouble, because trouble comes in many different ways, takes many different shapes and many different forms. But I'm thankful that You're a steady God, that you're a consistent God, that you're an immutable God, you don't change, You CAN'T change and You don't take on form, shapes, sizes and all of that, You are very consistent, and I thank You for that. I thank You that even when I am inconsistent Father God, You are so consistent.

I thank You for that Father God, I thank You Father God that You saturate me with Your very presence and that it's not always about a feeling because feelings come and go, but it's about a knowing Father God. I know that I know that I know I know that You are my very present help in times of trouble. That You are my shepherd that Psalms 23 talks about, the Lord IS my shepherd, I shall not want. You are my beginning; You are my middle and You are my end. You are my alpha and You are my omega, oh hallelujah, and everything in between, You are. You are a wonderful God, You are a faithful God, You are a comforting God and You are my deliverer.

I thank you Father God that Your love knows no bounds Father God. That Your love and Your presence cannot be put in a box Father God and it cannot be bound by time Father God. That You just as You came out of the grave, Father God, what I wanted to say is just as You busted out of that grave Father God, You bust out of the bounds and the boxes that we as human beings put you in. Father forgive us for putting You in a box and forgive us Father God for thinking that we know that we truly know at our core who You are and what you will do. Father I thank You that You love me and that You loved me so much Father God that long before I even was, You went to the cross for me.

Thank you, Father God, that even long before time, You knew me, You handpicked me. You handpicked every gift that You have put in me, every gift at the very core of my being, my personality Father God, You handpicked every part of it, and You knitted it together in my mother's womb. You made sure Father God, that I was handpicked for my family, that I fell number 5 of 6, because there was importance in that, that You allowed me Father God to marry the man I married and You allowed me Father God to meet all of the people that I have met. You allowed me to be the mother to the two sons that You gave me. You allowed me to be the grandmother to my two treasures and all the others that will come after them, Father God. YOU PICKED ME and I am so thankful for that Father God.

Your love knows no bounds and I am thankful Father God, I am thankful that even in my messiness, EVEN in my messiness, You knew me and STILL loved me. Even when people walk away from me, even when people do not get me, You STILL LOVE ME.

When everybody else walks away, You stay, You remain, You are faithful. You are a faithful God and You are faithful to the call that is on my life and I thank You for that. I thank You for that Father God.

So, Father, I'm thankful on this day, this beautiful day that You've given me, that this is the day the Lord hath made, I WILL, I WILL, I WILL rejoice, no matter my circumstances, no matter what's going on all around me. No matter the storms that are here and that are coming and will come, I WILL rejoice and be glad in it because I serve, I walk with, I love, I am anointed by an AMAZING God who HAND PICKED ME, in the name of Jesus I bless You Father God. Amen.

Jesus is Walking by...

Luke 18:41 (AMP)

Saying, What wilt thou that I shall do unto thee? And he said, Lord, that I may receive my sight.

I love the truth in the Word of God where Jesus is walking by and someone is healed. Jesus always attracted a crowd everywhere he went. Sometimes it was difficult to get close to him because of the crowd. However, Jesus was always walking by and with him came healing, love, compassion, lessons, rebuke, and truth.

As Jesus was walking near Jericho, a blind man by the name of Bartimaeus heard a large amount of noise. He asked someone what was going on and they told him Jesus of Nazareth was passing by. I can imagine that with all the BREATH AND AIR in his lungs Blind Bartimaeus cried out, "Jesus, Son of David, have mercy on me." The crowd rebuked him and said, "Be quiet." Have you ever had someone rebuke you as you cried out to God? Have you held your peace when everything in you screamed and cried out to God for_______?

Blind Bartimaeus cried out the more, "Thou Son of David, have mercy on me." At that moment Jesus stood still, commanded Bartimaeus to be brought to him, and asked him "What wilt thou that I shall do unto thee? "Blind Bartimaeus said "Lord, that I may receive my sight." Jesus did just that, because of Bartimaeus' faith.

Jesus is walking by. What do you need for Him to do on your behalf? Is your faith such that he can say, "It is done", or is your faith lacking? Jesus is walking by....

Father, thank You for just walking by. Father, increase my faith so that I may receive my _______. In Your Name I pray, Amen.

Blessings.

Impostors in your Fields & Gardens
Psalm 65:11(KJV)

Thou crownest the year with thy goodness; and thy paths drop fatness.

It is that time of year when people, as much as they are able due to the current state of our world, are returning to the fields and gardens. The large fields and gardens await the one who will work the land to produce a beautiful and bountiful harvest. The harvest can be anything from corn, beans, tobacco, to tomatoes, cucumbers and flowers. One thing fields and gardens have in common, is that the impostors will show up also.

An impostor could be a weed, insect or animal. When an impostor shows up the goal is destruction of the harvest. Our lives represent the fields and gardens. In our relationships: families, marriages, parenting, church and communities we set out to produce a beautiful and bountiful harvest. Yet always in the midst, are the impostors, waiting to destroy that which is planted.

The impostors can be sin, drugs, infidelity, separation, divorce, abuse and so much more. The impostors choke the life out of the harvest as the weed chokes the life out of the crop. Just as every plant is affected by the destruction of the impostor, so is every person, family, marriage, etc.

What are we to do? For the fields and gardens, we spray, we work the land, and we pull up weeds from the roots. For the family, marriage, community, etc., we surround them with prayer, the Word, boundaries and accountability. We take further steps and we reach out to those who are trained and set aside for the work of the harvest. What about you? Are you an impostor or a harvester? Do you create life or destroy life? Everyone has been an impostor sometime in life. The Word of God says in Romans 3:23, "for all have sinned and fallen short of the glory of God." Praise God that he made a way for us to shake of the impostor cloths and put on the clothes of harvesting and righteousness!

Father, help us to identify impostors when they come to our fields and gardens. Help us to identify them and dismantle them. Help us, Father, to set them on a path to harvest. Help us to evaluate ourselves to determine where we fall, as an impostor or a harvester. In Your Name I pray, Amen.

Blessings.

I Must Needs Go

John 4:4 (KJV)

And he must needs go through Samaria.

On His way to Galilee, Jesus felt it necessary to make a stop in the city of Samaria. Little did the people of Samaria realize, the Messiah was coming to their hearts and homes that day. His stopover was much bigger than anyone would know. His visit was far reaching and its effects are felt even today. You see, Jews and Samaritan's did not connect or befriend, nor would they be seen with each other. It was unheard of, until the necessity of going through Samaria changed that thought and impact. Jesus had a divine appointment with a Samaritan Woman at Jacob's Well. Little did she know, that her life would be forever changed, as would her village. Jesus offered the woman and all in her village, Living Water. The woman and many more were saved that day. The gospel himself brought salvation to the people of Samaria. When the disciples returned and found Jesus talking to the Samaritan woman, they thought Jesus had lost his mind. When he decided to stay for a couple of days, they were convinced he had lost it. Jesus was fully aware of what he was doing. There is an URGENCY IN THE GOING. Salvation awaited him in Samaria and he was not willing to allow anything or anyone to stop him from going. He was doing his Father's will. What about you? Where does your urgency take you? Who is waiting on you for that divine appointment? Are you willing to cross lines, races, barriers, and naysayers to do the Father's will? Father help us to sense the urgency to go and do the Father's will. Help us to say, "I must needs go." Amen.